POP
50+

Adam Wallace & Chris Kennett

DAD JOKES ARE THE

A Scholastic Australia Book

For Dad, in memory of the kid who only had ears!
Thank you for your jokes and your friendship—AW

To my dad, Colin.
Thanks for giving me your silly sense of humour! x—CK

Scholastic Australia
An imprint of Scholastic Australia Pty Limited
PO Box 579 Gosford NSW 2250
ABN 11 000 614 577
www.scholastic.com.au

Part of the Scholastic Group
Sydney • Auckland • New York • Toronto • London • Mexico City
• New Delhi • Hong Kong • Buenos Aires • Puerto Rico

Published by Scholastic Australia in 2022.

NATIONAL LIBRARY OF AUSTRALIA

A catalogue record for this book is available from the National Library of Australia

ISBN: 978-1-76112-316-0

Typeset in Portada Text, featuring Helenita Book Rough and PhysEd.

Design by Nicole Stofberg.

Printed in China by RR Donnelley.

Scholastic Australia's policy, in association with RR Donnelley, is to use papers that are renewable and made efficiently from wood grown in responsibly managed forests, so as to minimise its environmental footprint.

10 9 8 7 6 5 4 3 2 23 24 25 26 / 2

It's **Father's Day,** and my dad rocks.
He really is **the best!**

Except for his **terrible dad jokes . . .**

I wish he'd give them a rest.

The other day, as we left the house—
how's this for **really bad—**
Mum said she'd call him **later.** He said,

I give Dad flowers
as a gift; he does a
happy dance.

Then waters them
and says to me,

I groan and
shake my head.
Dad gives a
panicked shout.

'Don't shake
your head!'
he cries.

As we get ready for the beach,
Dad tells us about his dream,

where he went to a **haunted beach** and ate
sand-witches and **ice-screeeeeeeeeam!**

‘Can you make **me** a sandwich?’ I ask...
then quickly regret what I said.

‘You’re a sandwich!’ Dad cries,
holding **bread** against my head!

Finally, we're on our way,
and Dad **sings** as he drives along,

He thinks it's **super** funny
to sing every single word **wrong!**

Dad says, starting to drive faster.

'Where?' I say. 'Too late!' he cries.

'We've already gone **pasta!'**

Mum asks Dad the time.
'Time for a new **watch,'** he says with glee.

And as soon as we get to the beach he shouts,

He buys a drink, and the server asks,
'Want that drink **in a bag?'**

'No, thanks,' Dad says. 'Leave it **in the bottle.'**
My shoulders start to sag.

We dig in the sand, then I say, 'I'm hot!'
'Hi, Hot,' is Dad's reply.

Dad's jokes make me want to cry.

'Anyway,' he adds, 'it's good to be hot.
Hot's **faster** than cold, for sure.
I know this 'cause you can **catch** a cold.'

‘Please, Dad,’ I beg.

‘NO MORE!’

Mum says I need a haircut when my fringe hangs down too far.

'Guess how **sheep** get haircuts?' Dad asks. 'They visit the **BaaaaaBaaaaaa!**'

It's nearly time to head on home,
so we search rock pools for fish.
Dad's sure crabs won't share their pools,
because they are **shellfish!**

On the way back to the car,
Dad turns to us with a sigh.

'The ocean will **really** miss us.
Look at it **wave** goodbye.'

And even as we're driving home,
Dad is still **chatting** away.
'Hey, kids! Would you come to the beach
if it wasn't a **SUNday?'**

That night, Dad tucks me into bed
and says **he'll love me forever.**
Every day's his **favourite**
when we are all **together.**

I know that all of Dad's jokes are

super, super bad . . .

But that's one reason **I love him,**

because it's part of what makes him

my dad!

POP
50+
POP
50+
50+
POP
POP
50+